JF BAY

KU-504-694

UNIVERSITY OF WALES COLLEGE NEWPORT
LIBRARY
AND
LEARNING
RESOURCES
CAERLEON
★

Caerleon
Library

$SARAH$ and the $SANDHORSE$

Story by Andrew Baynes
Pictures by Michael Foreman

A

Andersen Press · London

Text copyright © 1994 by Andrew Baynes. Illustrations copyright © 1994 by Michael Foreman.

The rights of Andrew Baynes and Michael Foreman to be identified as the author and illustrator of this work have been asserted by them in accordance with the Copyright, Designs and Patents Act, 1988.

First published in Great Britain in 1994 by Andersen Press Ltd., 20 Vauxhall Bridge Road, London SW1V 2SA. Published in Australia by Random House Australia Pty., 20 Alfred Street, Milsons Point, Sydney, NSW 2061. All rights reserved. Colour separated in Switzerland by Photolitho AG, Offsetreproduktionen, Gossau, Zürich. Printed and bound in Italy by Grafiche AZ, Verona.

10 9 8 7 6 5 4 3 2 1

British Library Cataloguing in Publication Data available.

ISBN 0 96264 476 3

This book has been printed on acid-free paper

One summer's morning in St Ives, Sarah awoke in her room by the sea. Looking out of her window she could see her friend the artist. He was already at work down on Porthgwidden beach, sculpting a horse in the sand.

Sarah got dressed quickly, picked up Honey, her favourite toy horse and hurried down to the beach.

Sarah loved horses. Her greatest wish was to have a horse of her own but she knew she was much too small. So instead, she patted the Sandhorse, and pretended that it was real.

When the Sandhorse was finished the artist settled down to eat his sandwiches. He and Sarah fed the sparrows that flocked to join them. They spent a happy day together.

As the sun went down, the artist collected his things and set off
for home. Sarah was already tucked up in bed – but she could

not sleep. It was a cold, windy night. Sarah was worried about the Sandhorse lying all alone on the beach.

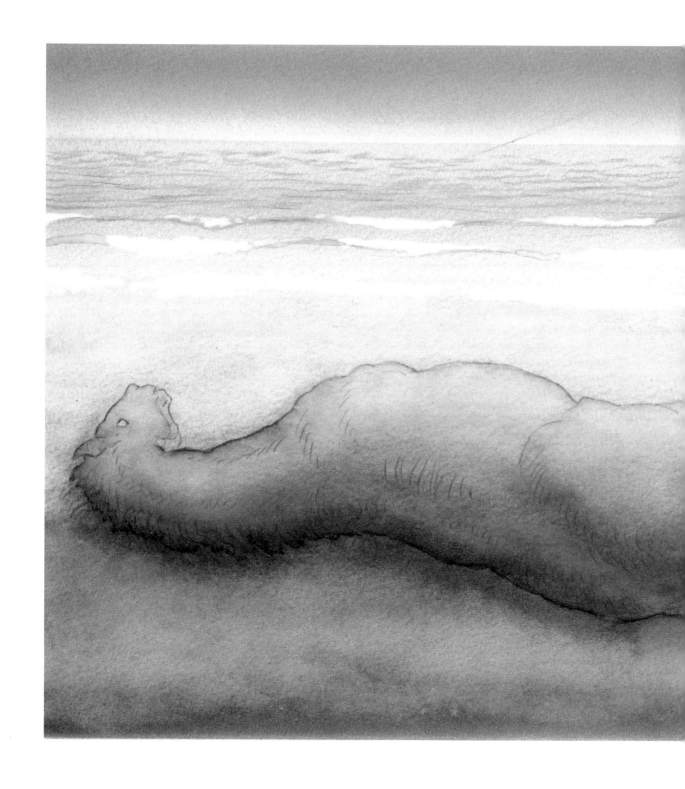

So, she picked up her patchwork blanket and crept down to where

the Sandhorse lay. In the moonlight it looked almost alive.

She knelt down and whispered into the Sandhorse's ear. "Poor Sandhorse, you must be so cold and lonely," she said. "I've brought my blanket to keep you warm."

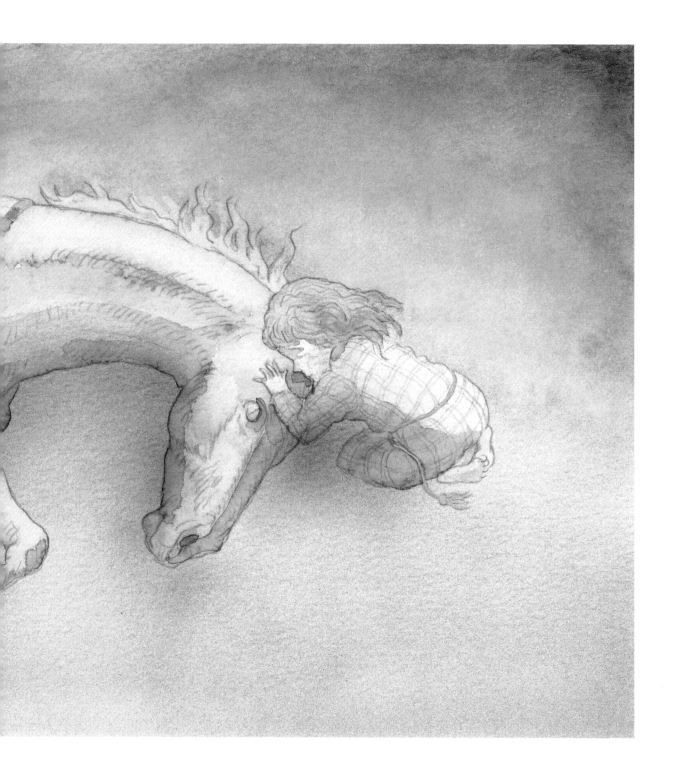

Sarah laid the blanket over the Sandhorse and curled up beside it. She did not mean to stay for long but she was so tired that she fell fast asleep.

That night, Sarah dreamed that she was galloping across the sea on a golden horse. The hooves chimed like bells as they splashed through the waves.

"What kind of horse are you?" she asked. The horse tossed its head.
"Don't you recognise me?" said the Sandhorse. "I am the one
you cared for."
"Sandhorse, it's really you," she cried.

Just then, Sarah remembered Honey.
"We've forgotten Honey," she cried, but the Sandhorse had already turned back. It was as though he knew what Sarah was thinking.

As they approached the town, she saw Honey waiting at her window. Honey leapt for joy as she saw them and in a swish of the Sandhorse's tail, all Sarah's toy horses were set free.

"Hold on, Sarah!" said the Sandhorse. Sarah clung tightly to the mane as they galloped across the bay, racing dolphins on the way.

Round and round the lighthouse they went, faster and faster until they began to fly.

Sarah looked down at the lights of old St Ives twinkling below.

"I must be dreaming," she thought.
"Your dream is a magical world," cried the Sandhorse.

They flew over high cliffs, hills and shining rivers. Wild ponies

on the moors pranced as Sarah and the Sandhorse flew overhead.

Higher and higher they climbed up into the night sky. They flew through the clouds, towards the stars of Pegasus, to a land

of magical horses, a place where the Sandhorse could live
forever.

As the sun rose the next morning the artist returned to the
beach for another day with the Sandhorse. But the Sandhorse

was not there. All he could see was Sarah asleep and hoofprints leading out towards the sea.

Caerleon
Library